BREIGHTMET
01204 332352

Bolton
Council

IBC 12\5\22
→ CL

D1313338

Please return/ renew this item
by the last date shown.
Books can also be renewed at
www.bolton.gov.uk/libraries

JYR

BOLTON LIBRARIES

BT 2128729 5

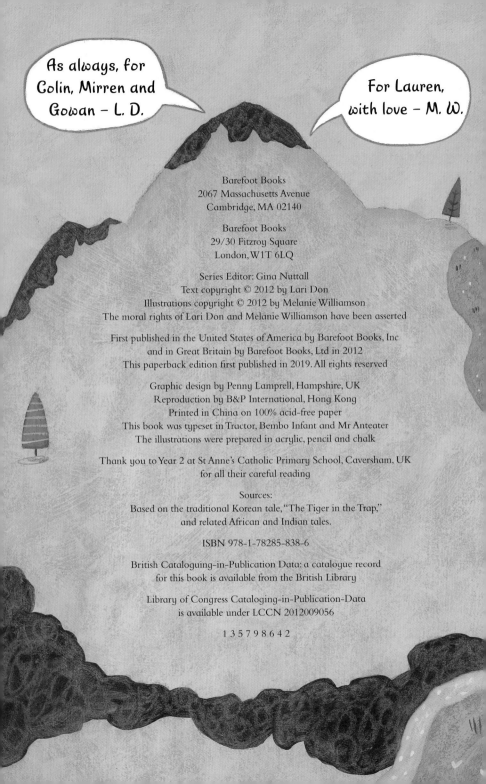

As always, for Colin, Mirren and Gowan – L. D.

For Lauren, with love – M. W.

Barefoot Books
2067 Massachusetts Avenue
Cambridge, MA 02140

Barefoot Books
29/30 Fitzroy Square
London, W1T 6LQ

Series Editor: Gina Nuttall
Text copyright © 2012 by Lari Don
Illustrations copyright © 2012 by Melanie Williamson
The moral rights of Lari Don and Melanie Williamson have been asserted

First published in the United States of America by Barefoot Books, Inc
and in Great Britain by Barefoot Books, Ltd in 2012
This paperback edition first published in 2019. All rights reserved

Graphic design by Penny Lamprell, Hampshire, UK
Reproduction by B&P International, Hong Kong
Printed in China on 100% acid-free paper
This book was typeset in Tractor, Bembo Infant and Mr Anteater
The illustrations were prepared in acrylic, pencil and chalk

Thank you to Year 2 at St Anne's Catholic Primary School, Caversham, UK
for all their careful reading

Sources:
Based on the traditional Korean tale, "The Tiger in the Trap,"
and related African and Indian tales.

ISBN 978-1-78285-838-6

British Cataloguing-in-Publication Data: a catalogue record
for this book is available from the British Library

Library of Congress Cataloging-in-Publication-Data
is available under LCCN 2012009056

1 3 5 7 9 8 6 4 2

Never Trust a Tiger

A Tale from Korea

Retold by **Lari Don**

Illustrated by **Melanie Williamson**

Barefoot Books
step inside a story

Contents

CHAPTER 1

The Tiger in the Pit

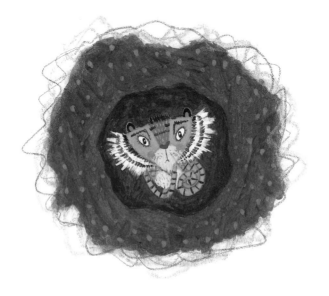

"Help! Help me!"

Only one person heard the cry for help.

He was a merchant on his way to market.

He was carrying his pack of spices along a

mountain path.

"Help! Get me out of here!"

The merchant looked all around.

Who was calling for help? There was no

one there. Then he saw a deep pit at the

side of the path. At the bottom of the pit

was a tiger!

It was the most beautiful tiger he had ever seen.

The tiger said, "Please help me! I've fallen into this pit and I can't escape. I'm hungry and thirsty and a bit scared."

The tiger put his huge paws together
and begged, "Please help me out of this pit
and I will never forget your kindness!"

The merchant thought it was wrong
to trap something so bright and beautiful
in such a dark place. So he agreed to help
the tiger escape.

He found a fallen tree and dragged
it over to the pit. He yelled, "Watch out
below!" and kicked one end of the tree
trunk down into the hole.

The tiger jumped to the side as the
tree trunk fell down. The trunk was very
long. So, when one end hit the bottom, the
other end was still sticking up into the air.
It leaned on the edge of the pit. It was now
a ramp, leading out of the pit.

The tiger climbed up the tree trunk
slowly. He reached the top and jumped off
onto the ground. He stretched his paws out
in front of him and bent his back low.

He flicked his stripy tail and smiled.

"It's good to be out of that hole!"

The merchant smiled too. He was happy to have done a good deed. They smiled at each other.

Then, suddenly, the tiger jumped at the merchant's chest!

He knocked the merchant onto his back. Then the tiger opened his mouth wide. His long sharp teeth were right above the merchant's face.

Oh no!

CHAPTER 2

The Argument

"It's good to be out of that hole,"
growled the tiger. "It's going to be even
better to eat you!"

"Eat me?" gasped the merchant.
"Why would you eat me? I saved you!"

"So you did. But I'm out now, so I don't need you to save me again. And I'm hungry, so I'm going to eat you."

"But that's not fair!"

The tiger smiled. "I don't want to be fair. I only want to be full!"

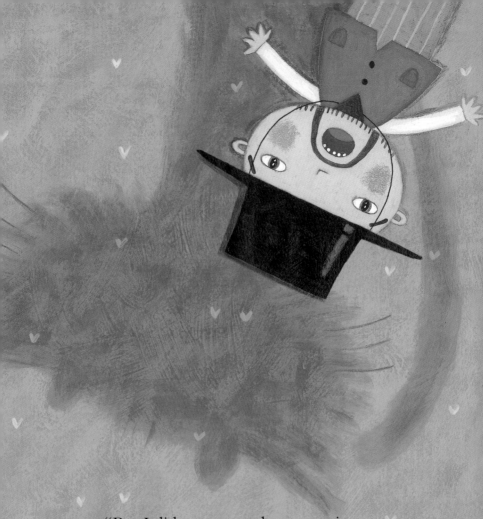

"But I did you a good turn, getting
you out of the pit. You can't repay good
with bad. Good deeds should be followed
by good deeds, not bad deeds…"

The tiger sighed. "All this arguing
is giving me a sore tummy. Please stop
talking and be quiet so I can eat you
in peace."

"No, I won't be quiet. This isn't fair.
You can't follow a good deed with a
bad deed."

"I'm a tiger. I'm big. I have sharp teeth.
I can do what I like. Now be quiet."

The merchant thought. "All right.
I'll be quiet and let you eat me in peace,
but…"

"Thank you," the tiger said loudly
before the merchant had finished speaking.

"But only if we let someone else sort out the argument," the merchant said. "I'll stop arguing when someone else judges whether it's fair that bad deeds can follow good deeds."

"Who could we get to judge?" asked the tiger.

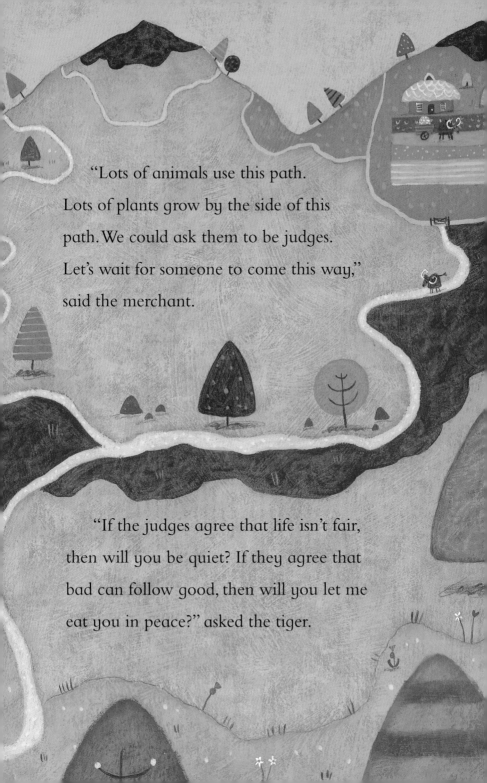

"Lots of animals use this path. Lots of plants grow by the side of this path. We could ask them to be judges. Let's wait for someone to come this way," said the merchant.

"If the judges agree that life isn't fair, then will you be quiet? If they agree that bad can follow good, then will you let me eat you in peace?" asked the tiger.

"Yes," agreed the merchant.

So the merchant lay on the ground, with the tiger crouching on his chest. And they waited.

An ox stomped towards them.

Bother!

CHAPTER 3

The Ox's Answer

The merchant said, "Please, Ox, can you help us settle an argument?"

"I can try," said the ox slowly, as he chewed some grass.

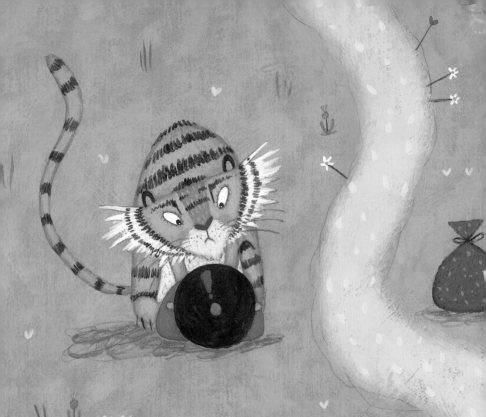

So the tiger told the ox the story of
how he had been in the pit. The merchant
told the story of how he had rescued the
tiger. The tiger said he was now planning
to eat the merchant. The merchant said
that was not fair, because you could not
follow a good deed with a bad deed.

The ox thought and he chewed.
The ox chewed and he thought. After
a long time, he said, "Life's not fair."
The tiger grinned and licked
his teeth. But the ox had not finished.

"In my life," the ox said, "good deeds are not followed by good deeds. I have worked for my master for many years," he went on.

"When I am too old to work, my master will send me to the butcher. Then I will be killed and eaten. All my good work will be followed by a bad end. So bad can follow good. Tigers can eat their rescuers."

The tiger smiled wider. He lowered
his teeth to the merchant's neck, as the ox
stomped off.

"Wait!" said the merchant. "That
was only one animal! We have to ask
someone else."

"Then will you be quiet and let
me eat you in peace?" asked the tiger.

"Yes, if the next judge agrees that it's fair," the merchant said.

So the merchant lay on the ground, with the tiger crouching on his chest. And they waited.

I'm very hungry.

29

CHAPTER 4

The Tree's Answer

The pine tree above them swayed in the wind. The merchant said, "We could ask the tree."

So the tiger called up, "Pine Tree, can you help us sort out an argument?"

"I can try," said the pine tree,
bending its branches down to listen.

The merchant and the tiger both
told their sides of the story.

Tweet! Tweet!

"So," said the tiger, "tell this foolish merchant that life isn't fair. Tell him that bad can follow good."

The pine tree said, "But in my life good has always followed good. I let the birds make nests and bring up their baby birds in my branches."

The pine tree went on, "Then the birds carry the seeds from my cones for miles, so that my baby trees grow all over these mountains. The more good I do for the birds, the more good they do for me. So life can be fair, and tigers should not eat their rescuers."

As the tree creaked upright again, the merchant grinned at the tiger. "Off you get, then!"

The tiger said, "But the ox said I should eat you."

The merchant said, "The tree said you shouldn't."

They looked at each other. The tiger
said, "One said yes, the other said no. They
haven't sorted out our argument at all."

The merchant nodded. "We need one
more judge to sort out our argument."

So the merchant lay on the ground, with the tiger crouching on his chest. And they waited.

CHAPTER 5

The Hare's Question

A big grey hare hopped along the
path. The merchant and the tiger both said,
all in a rush, "Hare! Hare! Can you please
help us sort out our argument?"

The hare said she would try.

The tiger and the merchant told
their stories at the same time. The tiger
explained how he fell into the pit. The
merchant explained how he helped the
tiger. The tiger told the hare how he
attacked the merchant. The merchant
said how unfair it was.

They both said, "So please tell us, is it fair that bad deeds should follow good deeds? Or should good always be repaid by good?"

The hare said, "Slow down! I can't understand when you're both talking at the same time!"

So they both tried to tell her again.

When they had finished, the hare said, "Let me see if I've got this right. The merchant was in the pit and the tiger was up a tree…"

"No, no, no!" they both shouted. And they tried to tell the story again.

The hare shook her head. "I'm sorry.
I can't understand this at all. You will have
to show me rather than tell me. Where
were you both when all this started?"

CHAPTER 6

Back to the Start

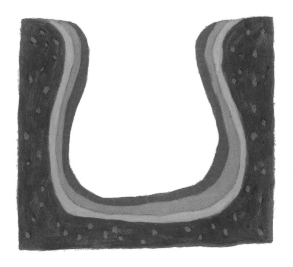

"I was in the pit," said the tiger.

"I was on the path," said the merchant.

"Please show me where you were,"
said the hare.

They looked at each other.

Then the tiger climbed off the
merchant and jumped back into the pit.
The merchant stood up and stretched.

"Was that tree trunk in the pit when
you met?" asked the hare.

"No," said the tiger and merchant together.

"Then take the trunk out," said the hare.

So the tiger pushed and the merchant pulled. Together they heaved the trunk out of the pit.

Now the tiger was back in the pit, with no way out.

The hare looked at the merchant. "Do you still want my advice?"

The merchant nodded.

"I think you should just leave the tiger in the pit."

Come back!

The hare started to hop away.

The merchant shouted after her, "But...

But... was it fair? Should a good deed

always follow a good deed?"

The hare smiled. "That all depends

on who you help!"

The merchant picked up his pack
of spices and walked away from the pit.
He said to himself, "I'll never trust a tiger
again."

And the tiger sat in the pit, saying to
himself, "I wonder who I can ask to help
me out next?"